TODAY'S LESSON:
BLACK LIVES MATTER

WILLIE D. JONES

Will the Wordsmith Publications
MIDDLETOWN, NEW YORK

Will the Wordsmith Publications
P.O. Box 46
Middletown, New York 10940
www.willthewordsmith.com

Publisher's Note: This is a work of fiction. Names, characters, places, and incidents are a product of the author's imagination. Locales and public names are sometimes used for atmospheric purposes. Any resemblance to actual people, living or dead, or to businesses, companies, events, institutions, or locales is completely coincidental.

Today's Lesson: Black Lives Matter/ Willie D. Jones. -- 1st ed.
ISBN 978-0-9987304-1-7

BISAC: FIC049000

The issues raised in this book are deeply personal to me. It was an exercise that helped me work through my feelings regarding something similar that happened to one of my sons. Thankfully, I was able to respond to his teacher's ill-considered rhetoric about the shooting death of Michael Brown in Ferguson, Missouri, in writing and by telephone. But that situation made me wonder just how many of my son's classmates had anyone at home to put the events surrounding the death of Michael Brown—and Tamir Rice, and Eric Garner, and John Crawford, and Ezell Ford, and Akai Gurley, and Walter Scott, and Freddie Gray, and Philando Castile, and Alton Sterling, and dozens of others—in proper context. How many other parents reacted by contacting the teacher and the principal and letting them know, in no uncertain terms, that teachers should not be in the business of endorsing police brutality and state-sanctioned murder? It was my desire to respond, not only for me and my son, but for us all. With that in mind, I began writing this story.

I'd like to dedicate this work to the twin apples of my eye, my sons, Aaron and Jaden. I love you guys more than you'll ever know. I'm committed to making the world better for you and your children.

"He has shown you, O mortal, what is good. And what does the LORD require of you? To act justly and to love mercy and to walk humbly with your God."

–MICAH 6:8

Acknowledgements

I couldn't have completed this without the contributions of several people who sowed into this project with their time, insights, and expertise: Nicole McFarlane and Nicholas Rodriques, for helping make the two main characters come alive; Samuel K. Moore, for a critical early-stage reading; my friends at the Cornwall Writers Circle (with special thanks to Steve Otlowski and Catharine Tomlins), for helpful questions and advice; Felicia Murrell, for her keen editing eye; Beatrix Susan Saavedra Doyle, the wonderful artist who blew me away with the image that appears on the book's cover; and Mark Montgomery, for invaluable help with the cover design.

Today's Lesson: Black Lives Matter

"Good afternoon, Mr. Carter." The woman behind the security desk eyeballed his driver's license. "What brings you here this time of day?"

"Good question. I'll let you know when *I* find out. I got a call from my wife an hour ago telling me that I needed to get here as soon as humanly possible. She's not the melodramatic type, so I figure it must be serious. I need to see the principal and find out just what went awry today."

He accepted the adhesive label with his name, Cedric Carter, handwritten beneath the school's Hamilton East High School Fighting Tigers logo. He stuck it to the lapel of his suit jacket, then took a deep breath before heading off in the direction of the main office.

"Is this your dad?" came a voice from behind the desk as he stepped through the office door. "He's gonna be absolutely disgusted with your behavior."

And just like that, the part of Cedric that was quick to shut down someone verbally—sometimes with ruthless intensity—was at war with what he called his "corporate negro" alter ego, the one who always maintained his polished professional demeanor and sanitized language.

"Yes, I'm his father," Cedric said to the woman. "And you are?"

"I'm the office manager."

Another woman, seated at a desk five feet behind her left shoulder, rolled her eyes, knowing that her office secretary job didn't have a single bit of management authority built in.

"Well, I'm here to see Principal Fortson, but I'm going to sit over here and talk to my son for a minute. Then I'll decide for myself whether to be disgusted or not."

"Suit yourself," she said.

Cedric could tell that his son, Marcus, had been crying. He gave the boy—who, at a shade below six feet, was one growth spurt away from looking at him eye to eye—a long hug and reassured him that everything would be all right. Even as they embraced, tears began to flow down Marcus's cheeks again.

"Come on. Sit, son. Tell me what happened."

"*I'll* tell you what happened," said the self-appointed "office manager." She leaned forward as if she were speaking into a microphone and said, "He threatened his chemistry teacher. And I think he hit her, too, which means his goose is cooked. I mean, how are these kids supposed to learn anything at all if they don't have an ounce of self-control?"

"Excuse you?" Cedric said.

"I mean, the mouth on him," she said, gathering a stack of papers together for stapling. "I wouldn't be surprised if he gets sent home and told never to come back."

Cedric took another deep breath, then fixed his most steely gaze on her.

You glorified form stamper and packet maker. If you don't go somewhere with yo' self-entitled behind. All up in my ass and don't know shit. Your only safe move on this checkerboard is to let Dr. Fortson know I'm here, then keep it pushin'.

But Cedric kept the words to himself.

Although the thought hit the bullseye dead center, he knew that checking the woman behind the desk for her loud-mouthed arrogance would only serve to paint him as just another angry black man, disqualified from being treated with dignity.

Hold it together, Cedric, he told himself. *Wear the mask.*

He opted for the more politically correct approach. "Well, I'll just wait for Dr. Fortson to arrive so that the people in the classroom, who actually witnessed whatever transpired there, can give their sides of the story."

"His side of the story? Please. You might wanna go ahead and have a serious talk with him about how a *real* man treats a lady."

"Well, thank you for that bit of unsolicited advice," Cedric said.

3

While she continued blathering on, he fought back the urge to let the woman have it with both barrels. *Why does she insist on coming for me when I haven't sent for her? She must be related to the chick who we just let go at my office because she felt deputized to be all up in everything except the work she was paid to do. Where do they make these people? There must be a factory somewhere. I need to remember to Google that.*

Meanwhile, Marcus was listening to the secretary's scolding drone, thinking, *Bruh! Do you know just how close you are to getting dragged right now? Pops is not here for the games.*

Marcus was well aware that Cedric Carter, Esq. was not in the habit of taking any shorts or slights. And he could tell by the look on his father's face that he wanted to snap off verbally, but had reined himself in.

Cedric, finally at the end of his patience with the woman's "If I were king for a day" speech, interrupted her mid-sentence. "You need to hit your turn signal, check your mirrors, and ease back into your lane before you crash. Regardless of what you have convinced yourself, I'm here to see Dr. Fortson and nobody else."

"Well, she's not here," the woman said in a huff, "and I'm not sure when she'll be back."

"We'll wait. Thank you for *all* your help."

The secretary, fully clued in to the fact that she had better put an end to her Judge Judy moment, couldn't seem to figure out what to do next.

Cedric turned his back to her and gave his full attention to Marcus. "So, you were about to tell me why I'm here."

"Look, Dad. I'm sorry. I just—"

"Start from the beginning."

"*I was in my fifth period AP chemistry class and we were talking about how chemicals that by themselves are inert can be combined to create powerful explosions. Somebody said they wanted to make some bombs so they could drop them on the cops who killed Tamir Rice. That's when Miss Orenstein, my chemistry teacher, went smooth off.*

She said, *"You think that's funny? How dare you?! The police have a tough enough job as it is without you people bellyaching about the way they fight crime. You should be thankful that they're willing to put their lives on the line every day to try to put the awful thug element behind bars where they belong."*

I asked her a simple question. "Do you think Tamir Rice, a twelve-year-old boy outside playing in the park, was a thug?"

That's when she killed it, Dad.

She said, "Look. All I know is that he invited trouble and now people are rioting and looting because he got what he asked for."

5

So I said, "You mean going to the park to play was him asking to get killed? You know that doesn't make ANY kind of sense, right?"

Peep this, Dad. You won't believe this part. *She had the nerve to tell me, "Put yourself in their shoes. They see a gun... What are they supposed to think?"*

I'm sorry, but she had to get got. So, I cut her to shreds. *I said, "They're actually supposed to think. But they didn't. They didn't think about what they were doing until after he was lying on the ground dying and they were trying to find needle and thread to knit together a story to make it okay that they murdered a little boy, in broad daylight, only a few feet from the teeter-totter."*

She came back with, "So says you. You weren't there and neither was I."

Then I told her, "And here you are, saying it was Tamir's fault that the police pulled a drive-by. That's why people are out here shouting Black Lives Matter. Because people like you act like you don't get it. You look at Tamir—and the other black people who get hemmed up by the police for something stupid like having a tail light out or for nothing at all—and say, 'Oh well. Fine by me.' You know that's racist, right?"

Of course, the class was like, "OOOOOOOH"

This one girl said, "Daaaamn, Marcus. Tell us what you really think."

Miss Orenstein stopped me right there. "Wait. Who are you calling racist? How dare you!"

I said, "Well, if the white privilege fits..."

She was hotter than the skin between a fat man's thighs. *She said, "Don't demonize me just because I happen to think a thriving society is built on law and order!"*

I said, "Well, this society must not be thriving, 'cause it was built on the backs of black people, not law and order. If there was law and order, there wouldn't have been thousands of lynchings, rapes, beatings, bombings, cross burnings... I could go on. But now that we're not available for free labor, and won't sit quietly for white terrorism, people like you want to call us thugs and make it okay to shoot us down like dogs."

Can you believe she had the nerve to say, *"Oh, just stop it! Excuse after excuse after excuse. When the police tell you to put your hands up, put 'em up. When they tell you to stop resisting, stop it already!"*

I was done. No sense in holding back at that point. *I said, "Wow... You know what's the worst part about your type of racist? You're so fake about it. You get up every morning and come here to get a check, on some 'Hey this is just my hustle, not my life.' Be honest. You couldn't care less whether half the people in this room live or die."*

Cedric's raised eyebrows gave away his surprise at Marcus's outburst. "Wow! You went all the way there, huh?"

"Yeah. *That's when somebody in the class said, "AWKWARD."*

I said, "I know, right?"

Then, she told me to get out.

I was like, "For what? I haven't done anything. Nothing but help you expose yourself for who you really are. You're welcome."

That's when it got ugly. Now, she's probably, like, ninety-five pounds with rocks in her pockets. But she came from the front of the room, all the way over to where I was and stood over me like that was supposed to put fear in my heart. She started screaming in my face.

"GET OUT OF MY ROOM! NOW! You wanna be disrespectful? We'll see how you like it when you're sitting home on suspension. And you're right. I'll still be getting a check—whether you learn or not."

I didn't even look at her.

I said, "You might as well take that 'L' I just handed you and get back to the regularly scheduled program already in progress."

Then she grabs my arm like she was gonna physically—I don't know—maybe drag me out of the room. The whole class busted out laughing at how pathetic she looked. I'm guessing she looked sort of like when I was four or five and you would pick me up in the air, and I would turn right around and say, 'Now let me pick you up, Daddy!' And you'd stand there while I wrapped my arms around your legs and struggled and strained and ended up doing nothing but wrinkling your pants.

I pulled my arm away and she lost her balance. Talk about mad? She stomped back up to the front of the room and wrote something on a piece of paper. Then she told this girl, Sarah, to take her little note to the principal's office.

Five minutes later, Mr. Grodski, the dean, came in like Thor without the hammer. He did his usual: standing with his arms folded so the muscles in his forearms will bulge. That's why he always wears that short sleeve shirt and sweater vest combo that looks like he's about to go apply for the assistant manager position at Arby's. Anyway, that's his 'Drill Sergeant' position. Kids around here know that when he strikes The Pose, somebody's about to get dealt with.

At that point, Miss Orenstein got right to hyping him up, whining about how disruptive I was and how, "I try and try... I sit up at night, preparing good, exciting lessons so I can teach these kids something. And what's the thanks I get? Shouted down in the middle of the class period and my arm nearly yanked out of the socket by an angry, immature ruffian with no impulse control."

Of course, Grodski was more than ready to dance to the song she was singing. Apparently, he thought I hit her. So, he turned on his bullhorn voice and threatened to call the police on me if I didn't go with him to the office.

He said, "LET'S GO! RIGHT NOW! YOU'RE ALREADY IN HOT WATER, MISTER. ASSAULTING A TEACHER ON SCHOOL GROUNDS? WHAT A JACKASS. I THINK YOU KNOW WHAT WOULD'VE HAPPENED IF YOU'D TRIED THAT WITH ME.

COME ON, TOUGH GUY! CHOP-CHOP! IF I HAVE TO TELL YOU AGAIN, I'M GONNA CALL UP A BUDDY OF MINE WHO CARRIES A TASER AND CUFFS ON HIS BELT."

"I won't lie, Dad. I was low-key terrified. I wasn't even tryna see the police—not after last Saturday—so I grabbed my stuff and followed him out of the room. I guess he called Mom. She texted me and told me you were coming. I've been sitting here on this bench ever since."

*****

"Excuse me. Mr. Carter?"

"Yes."

"I'm Mark Grodski, the dean. I removed Marcus from the classroom after his altercation with his chemistry teacher, Miss Orenstein. Why don't you step into my office? Marcus, you can stay here while your dad and I try to iron this out."

"With all due respect... *Mr. Grodski*, is it? I'm going to need to speak with Dr. Fortson and Miss Orenstein in order to get to the bottom of what transpired here today. I don't see any point in hashing this out now, only to have to cover the same ground with them."

Cedric didn't bother to voice his thought: *Besides, there's nothing we're going to discuss that doesn't directly involve Marcus, so he'll be present and empowered to speak for himself when we sit down at the table with the two of them.*

Grodski couldn't believe his ears. Without even thinking about it, he'd folded his arms and begun tightening and unclenching his fists so that the muscles in his forearms would ripple.

Marcus laughed until Cedric nudged him.

"Well, Dr. Fortson is off site right now," Grodski said. "And she has a meeting with the district superintendent that starts at 3:30, so I guess we'll have to schedule something for later in the week. In the meantime—"

"Wait. Let me stop you right there," Cedric interjected. "This is not a 'later in the week' situation. You threatened to call the police on my son, and I'm going to need this matter settled before the end of business today. As a matter of fact, I wouldn't mind at all if the superintendent sat in as well. We'll wait here while you contact Dr. Fortson and bring her up to speed."

"All due respect to *you*, Mr. Carter, but you don't get to adjust Dr. Fortson's schedule—especially when your child is on the verge of being suspended. And honestly, he could be facing a criminal case if Miss Orenstein can't be convinced not to pursue charges for assault."

Is he serious right now? Cedric said to himself. *We both know that if we were anywhere but here, he'd never step to me with all that bass in his voice.*

Cedric took a deep breath and counted to three before speaking.

"My position here hasn't changed from what it was yesterday or the day before. I'm still a concerned parent. And I'm here in the middle of the workday to speak with the school's chief administrator about a serious breach in the protocol that was supposed to protect my son, but sadly did not. This is a big problem, and it needs to be treated as such."

So, fold your arms and flex all you want, Cedric thought. *I just hope you can dial Dr. Fortson from that position.*

Without waiting for a reply, Cedric returned his attention to Marcus.

Grodski grew tired of hovering and stormed off, but not before telling the father and son that they should be prepared to clean out the boy's locker.

Without so much as a sideways glance, Cedric said, "We'll do what we must."

Cedric shook his head and said, "These are the people you deal with every day?"

Marcus shrugged.

"Well, don't sweat it, son. I've got this."

Cedric pulled out his phone and told Siri to "Dial Karen."

Damn, Cedric thought as he stood up and moved farther away from the reception desk and the loud-mouthed secretary who had been risking spinal injury craning her neck to overhear the conversation with Grodski. *She's about to kill herself trying to get a sip of the tea.*

"Hey, Karen," he said. "Listen, I've got a situation over here. I'm going to need you to call Judge Roberts' chambers and ask for an adjournment for the case I have on her court calendar this afternoon."

"No need," the more junior assistant district attorney said. "Defense counsel just called, not two minutes before you did, looking for a plea deal. He asked for a two-year sentence with credit for time served. I told him to get back to his client and wake him up to the fact that, although we believe his story that this was a prank gone wrong, someone lost their life as a direct result of his actions. He's got about an hour and a half left to get back to me and accept my offer of five years."

Cedric smiled. He was proud of his protégé. "That's exactly what I would've recommended. Good job."

"Thanks, boss. How's Marcus?"

"He's fine. But one of his teachers is accusing him of assaulting her. He says she initiated the contact; I believe him. But I know the school is prepared to accept the 'she said' over the 'he said.' That leaves me no choice but to take this chemistry teacher to the woodshed."

"Uh-oh. She doesn't have a clue, does she?"

"Not a one."

But she gon' learn today, he thought.

"Well, better her than me," Karen said. "I hope it all works out. Tell Marcus I said hi. I'll see you tomorrow."

"Yeah. I will. And hey, thanks again. Have a good evening."

Now I can focus all of my attention on this madness, Cedric thought as he went and sat beside his son.

After another moment, he stood up again and edged closer to a file cabinet near the door of the office. He went through his phone's contact list, dialed a number and listened impatiently as the phone rang."

"Cedric?" asked the voice on the other end of the line. "What's goin' on, brother?"

"Listen. I need you to get over here to Hamilton East by 3 o'clock. I can tell things here are about to go sideways, and I can't have that."

"I'm afraid to ask why you're up at the high school right now. I'm in the middle of something, but as soon as I wrap this up, I'm there."

After a pause, the person Cedric called for help said, "Okay, tell me. What do I need to know?"

"Marcus is in trouble. I'll fill you in on the rest when you get here."

"Roger that."

"Thanks, man."

"You got it." CLICK.

"Hey, Marcus." Cedric said from where he was standing. "Where's the men's room?"

"There's one right across the hall."

"I'll be right back. In the meantime, I want you to get started writing down everything you can recall about what happened before you got pulled out of class."

*****

Cedric stood at the sink washing his hands, and began to pray silently.

Father God, I come to you right now, asking for divine intervention on behalf of my son, Marcus. I'm a master at trading verbal jabs and commanding a room with my words. It's what I do. But bluster and bravado aside, I'm shook right now. Marcus's life is on the line. Expulsion? A criminal record? Even with me as his advocate, nothing's guaranteed. God, give me the right words to say. While I'm doing what I do, I need you to do what you do. You've proven that you can make a way out of no way. Prove it again. These and all other blessings I ask in the mighty and matchless name of Jesus Christ. Amen.

Cedric took a deep, cleansing breath, then wondered whether Marcus's twin brother Malcolm had gotten wind of what happened during fifth period chemistry.

The bell sounded, marking the end of the eighth period. Cedric plucked a piece of lint from his gleaming bald head, adjusted his purple and green necktie, and waded into the sea of humanity that clogged the hall because school had just let out for the day.

Even if Malcolm wasn't aware—which Cedric doubted, considering how quickly rumors spread in the halls of a high school—he'd be looking for his brother so they could ride their bikes over to the offices of the *Hamiltonian Times*, the weekly community newspaper where the twins worked after school.

Marcus took after his father, in that he loved books and studied the melody, rhythm, and rules of language in the same way that an instrumentalist listens to good music and absorbs the lessons taught by the masters. He was becoming a pretty capable writer and had shown flashes of brilliance as an editor of more seasoned writers' stories.

Malcolm had inherited his mother's creative gene. Long before he learned to read, he had demonstrated a remarkable talent for drawing objects from memory. And by the time he reached middle school, his richly detailed portraits had become highly sought after.

Malcolm had, over the course of a single year, dragged the *Hamiltonian Times*, run by a group of aging 1960s-era hippies, kicking and screaming into the twenty-first century. When he first arrived, he bluntly shared his assessment that, "It's a wonder that you ever get issues out the door with this Windows '65 setup you've got going here."

He completely revamped the paper's layout, and initiated a redesign aided by a switch from Microsoft Publisher and Corel Draw to Adobe InDesign, Photoshop, and other modern tools of the desktop publishing trade. He even pushed Mike Riezenman, the *Hamiltonian Times'* ponytail-and-hoop-earring-wearing publisher to switch from the paper's longtime printer to an outfit that offered better paper stock and four-color covers for a lower price than they had been paying.

The beauty of Malcolm's newfangled approach was illustrated by a 16-page special edition on the Black Lives Matter movement that he and his twin brother had hatched at the dinner table with their parents. The latest edition of the new and improved *Hamiltonian Times* had landed on local newsstands a week earlier.

*****

Cedric reentered the main office and, sure enough, Malcolm had homed in on his twin. But he was being shooed away by the same nosy secretary who had insisted on injecting herself into the situation. She was adamant that Marcus's troubles "don't concern you."

Marcus wished he could hit her with Willy Wonka's famous brush-off line: *I said good day!* But Cedric stepping up behind Malcolm was the rough equivalent. Without saying a word, he caused the secretary to switch back to silent mode.

"Hey, son. How was your day today?"

"Dad!" a surprised Malcolm said.

Cedric hugged the boy and said, "Better than your brother's, I hope."

"Uhhh, yeah. From what I hear, his afternoon was…extra."

"Yes. Apparently, it was quite dramatic."

"Right after sixth period, somebody in his chemistry class told me how suspect Miss Orenstein is and how Marcus gave her the business." Turning to his brother, Malcolm added, "I guess you lived up to your name today, Marcus Garvey Carter."

Marcus grinned and kept writing.

"I have no idea how long Marcus and I will be here waiting for the principal," Cedric told Malcolm. "So, why don't you head on over to the paper and we'll meet you later at home. Tell Connie she'll see Marcus tomorrow."

"You won't have to wait long," said Malcolm. He pointed at the door, directing his father's attention to the woman standing on the other side of the portal.

The principal, Dr. Fortson, stood like a smooth stone amid the roaring rapids of students making their afternoon escape from the school building. Even while answering another parent's question about an upcoming school orchestra performance, she gave high fives, issued warnings about too much horseplay, and offered congratulations to students who'd improved their academic performance or behavior.

She'd hardly gotten inside the office door when the secretary ran over to meet her.

She said, "I don't know if you heard, but—"

Fortson cut her off. "I've heard, Millie. If you would, please go and page Mr. Grodski and Miss Orenstein. Thanks."

Look at her, Cedric thought. *She couldn't wait to break that bit of news.*

He watched the secretary as she scrambled back to her desk so she could grab the telephone. *I know you're itching to call down the people you think will rain down vengeance on Marcus for standing his ground, and on me, for having the gall to resist chewing him out publicly just because you said so.*

Cedric's attention was redirected when the principal turned and extended her hand to shake his.

"Mr. Carter?" she asked. "Kat Fortson. Too bad we're meeting under these circumstances."

"I agree. It's good to finally meet you. I just wish I could say it was a pleasure, considering what we have to talk about."

"Please excuse me for a moment," Principal Fortson asked. "I ducked out of a district-wide planning meeting and I need to check on a calendar item and move it so I don't drop the ball. You know how it is."

"Sure," Cedric replied. "We're certainly not going anywhere."

At almost the instant Dr. Fortson disappeared into her office, Marcus nudged his dad and whispered, "That's Miss Orenstein."

When she walked past them without speaking, Cedric noticed two ballpoint pens sticking out of the curly, ash blonde hair that was tied back into a bun. She'd obviously stuck one in there for safekeeping, forgotten it, then put another in later.

"I guess we're invisible over here," Marcus said to his father.

Cedric shrugged. "We'll all have plenty to say when we get on the other side of that door."

If they were boxers, they would have been more comfortable. At least in that circumstance, the people in each corner would have a clear sense of what to do. The fighters would have been staying loose by shadowboxing, while the corner men offered last-minute instructions and prepped the things that might be needed should things go badly for their fighter. But in this arena, where the ropes were file cabinets and bulletin boards, the pre-fight rituals hadn't been established.

Miss Orenstein busied herself checking her mail. She took her time examining a piece of junk mail that had landed in her slot.

She's about to stare a hole through that leaflet, Cedric thought. *The secret to cold fusion must be written on it.*

Meanwhile Marcus was praying, *Please don't let them suspend me. I know I didn't do anything wrong, but Mom's gonna be about as calm as the Hulk if I get kicked out. And I'm not tryna hear her*

*mouth 'cause I didn't just keep my big mouth shut
and leave Miss Orenstein stuck on stupid.*

The chemistry teacher glanced at her watch for
the sixth time in ten minutes, then muttered under
her breath, "I hope this doesn't take too long. I've
got papers to grade, a lesson to plan, and more forms
to fill out."

Finally, the frosted glass door that read:

KATHRYN M. FORTSON, Ed.D.
PRINCIPAL

opened again and Fortson gathered the participants
in the ongoing drama into her office suite. She asked
them all to join her at a rectangular table for eight.
She sat at the head of the table and Cedric,
understanding the laws of power, sat in the chair at
the opposite end. He wanted to present himself as
someone with equal authority in the situation, rather
than as a subordinate to Fortson.

When Cedric directed Marcus to claim the chair
to his right, Fortson laughed and said, "You don't
have to sit so far away."

"We're fine right here," Cedric said, putting his
hand on Marcus's shoulder to short circuit the boy's
learned response to teachers asking students to
move closer to the front of the room.

Miss Orenstein had staked out a neutral position,
in the second of three chairs to Fortson's right.

The principal glanced at her watch. "Mr. Grodski must be outside the building, making sure dismissal goes smoothly and the stragglers don't get into too much mischief. Let's go ahead and get started without him."

"Fine by me," Cedric said.

Fortson put on her reading glasses and pulled a yellow manila folder from a dark brown accordion file.

"Let's see here," she said. She thumbed through the folder's contents. "Ah! Here we go. Disciplinary Record—Malcolm Xavier Carter."

"Wrong twin," Cedric informed her. "This is Marcus."

Fortson slammed the folder shut and closed her eyes in disgust before quickly regaining her composure.

"Alrighty then," she said out loud through the egg on her face. She excused herself from the table, poked her head out of the door, and in the tone of a parent frustrated that their child carries out instructions like a buggy computer program, asked Millie the secretary whether she'd thought it would be an interesting change of pace to put the wrong student's folder on her table. After explaining that it was Marcus, not Malcolm Carter, who was in the room, and assuring her—twice—that she was not mistaken about that, the principal paused for a beat to regain her composure and paint a smile on her face before returning to her seat.

Millie hustled into the room and swapped folders with Fortson, but didn't have the humility to appear even the least bit chastened.

What a clown, Marcus said to himself.

Fortson said, "Thank you, Millie. That'll be all for now." Baked into the expression on the principal's face was the sour fruit of a thousand disappointments.

Cedric, who had earned a law degree from Yale, but had earned the rough equivalent of a Ph.D. in reading faces and other body language as a kid growing up in the projects in Brooklyn, sniffed out the principal's attitude.

Note to self, Cedric thought. *She can't stand any of these people.* Looking at Miss Orenstein, he told himself, *I bet she'll toss homegirl over there right under the bus at the first sign that my cross-examination of her testimony is putting school leadership on blast too.*

"Okay. Let's try this again," Fortson said. She fished through the new folder—but not before double checking that its typewritten label said

"Marcus Garvey Carter—Student ID: 04185337"

Finding not a single entry on the sheet that served as a placeholder for Marcus's disciplinary record, Fortson chuckled. She asked, "How did you make it to the tenth grade and never get into trouble, not even once? You're too good to be true."

Marcus laughed out loud at the ridiculousness of the question.

Is she serious right now? the boy said to himself.

But Fortson thought Marcus was actually entertaining the unspoken premise of the question.

Cedric looked around in utter disbelief, as if he were searching for the cameras set up to record him being pranked. Realizing that Fortson was indeed serious, he responded.

"You say that as though you expected something different. What is it about him that makes his lack of a disciplinary record so astounding to you?"

"Well... it's... ah... nothing. What I mean to say is that even the best students sometimes act out of character."

The thoughts in Marcus's head were written all over his face. *Bruh! How stupid do we look? What you meant to say was 'How did a lil' nigga like you get this far without getting in trouble?'*

"So, all of your top students exhibit discipline problems?" Cedric asked the principal.

"Well, I don't have to tell you how rambunctious boys can be—even the best of them." Fortson said by way of explanation. "Take today's outburst for example."

"Today's 'outburst' was not an example of boyhood rambunctiousness," Cedric insisted. "It was a direct—and quite necessary—response to the words and actions of someone who should know better. So, when we're framing this, let's be sure not to crop out the primary focal point of the picture."

Miss Orenstein interjected, "I don't think I feel comfortable with you making this my fault. It's like you're sitting here calling my integrity into question."

"Now, Miss Orenstein..." Fortson said. "No one's trying to do that."

"Speak for yourself," Cedric quickly responded. He was ready to begin knocking the teacher off her equilibrium in the hope that he could get her riled up enough to unintentionally let some truth slip out. Cedric couldn't count the number of times in his court cases that he'd induced angry, "You can't handle the truth!" responses from people on the witness stand.

He pushed Orenstein's buttons. "I don't believe for a second that my son attacked you. So, if that means I'm calling your integrity into question—or your teaching acumen or your grip on reality—then that's where we are. And let's address the subject of you feeling comfortable. You're a chemistry teacher, so you know exactly what I mean when I say that I couldn't give 6.02×10^{-23} percent of a damn about your comfort level."

Marcus tried to hold in a snicker, but couldn't.

OMG! He thought. *No dad didn't just roll up some chemistry homework like a newspaper and smack Miss Orenstein across the face with it. He don't give a molecule's worth of damn about how comfortable she is.*

Cedric continued. "You know what I'm really concerned about? That moment when you felt comfortable enough to tell my son that if he were to encounter some trigger-happy policeman on the street, anything that befalls him—up to and including being riddled with bullets—is exactly what he deserves."

"That's not what I said," a red-faced Miss Orenstein shouted. "Don't you DARE sit here and lie!" she said pointing at Marcus.

"You can put the cap back on your phony outrage," Cedric said. "Neither of us is going to come undone because of that. Now, did you or did you not stand in the front of the classroom and tell the children in your charge that Tamir Rice invited trouble and that he ultimately got exactly what he asked for?"

I hope, for your sake, that the answer is no, Fortson thought as she leaned forward in nervous anticipation and looked directly in Miss Orenstein's reddening face.

"That's ridiculous!" Orenstein argued. "I was upset at one student's idiotic suggestion that the Cleveland police be bombed. Can you believe the nerve? And I don't have a problem telling you, just like I told your son and his classmates. The police have a tough enough job as it is, without people piling on—you know, calling their integrity, professionalism, and sanity into question."

Pointing at Marcus, she added, "The instant I said that, this one called me a racist."

"Well, are you?" Cedric asked.

"I certainly AM NOT!"

Yessss... Let that anger flow through you, Cedric thought. *It won't be long before you trip over your own tongue.*

Fortson gave Marcus the floor. "What do you have to say for yourself, young man?"

"Well... I'm not going to sit here and call Miss Orenstein a bold-faced liar, 'cause that would be disrespectful. So, I'll say that her memory is failing her. She not only told me that Tamir Rice got what he asked for, she went a step further asking me to put myself in the police officers' shoes. The only part she got right was me calling her a racist.

I didn't bring it up in class—mainly because I didn't want everybody asking me a million questions about it, but I know *exactly* how it feels to have a cop draw his gun on you and point it in your face for no reason.

Saturday night, not even a week ago, Malcolm and I wanted to go to the roadside ice cream place in Hamilton Heights. We all piled in Dad's new car, went over there, stood in that long line, and got our cones. We were heading back home, enjoying the ride with the top down. My mom was using her cone as a microphone to sing along with Beyonce when flashing lights came on behind us. Long story medium: Dad was assaulted with a nightstick. My mom had a gun put up to the side of her head. I had it pointed right between my eyes, and then we were all cuffed and treated like criminals."

As Marcus offered a *CliffsNotes* version of the incident, he couldn't help reviewing the mental images that were seared into his memory.

Cedric had pulled over, fished his wallet out of his pocket, and asked Marcus's mom Jaclyn to pass him the registration and proof of insurance so he could have all of it on the dashboard by the time the officer approached the window.

From the backseat, Marcus recognized the steps his father was taking. Ever since he and Malcolm started taking Driver's Ed, Cedric would randomly quiz them on what they should do if they were ever pulled over. And, he did everything he'd been preaching to the boys. He kept his hands on the steering wheel at ten and two, with his fingers spread. He addressed the officer in a calm, even tone, like he was arriving at someone's house for a picnic; and he told the officer everything he was going to do before he did it.

But the cop was on READY... SET... and it didn't take much to get him hyped up. He was asking Cedric a bunch of questions, "Where ya headed? Is this your car? How long have you had it?"

Then he hit on the right question—the one that gave him and his partner what they thought was a good reason to pull their weapons out. He said, "You mind stepping out of the car for me, so we can take a look around and make sure you're not carrying anything on the naughty list?"

He said it real neighborly, like he was asking to borrow a rake or a cup of sugar. But he, his partner, and all four people in the car knew it wasn't really a request. When Cedric told him that he didn't consent to unlawful searches and he saw no reason to step out of the car, that was it.

Refusal of the officer's request to exit the vehicle was clearly an affront to the cop's sense of the natural order of things. The officer looked across the car at his partner—who was standing on the passenger side with his hand on his holster—and said, "Well, would you look at what we got here, Trent? We got ourselves a lawyer... knowing all his civil rights and shit. Isn't that nice?"

Then he leaned on the side mirror so he was basically up in Cedric's face.

"So, where'd you go to law school, Mr. Civil Rights Attorney? Mr. A-C-L-Youuuu?"

He damn near fell to the ground when Cedric said, "Yale University. And among the many things I learned there were the basics of the Constitution's Fourth Amendment protections against searches and seizures except in a very limited and clearly defined set of circumstances. And just as a little FYI, this is not one of those instances where a search is warranted." Then Cedric said, "See what I did there? Search? Warrant?"

The policeman exploded.

Later that night, the twins' grandfather—a retired police captain who had been tight with the cop who eventually rose through the ranks to become the chief of police ever since their days as young beat cops—came by the house to get chapter and verse on what happened.

The elder Mr. Carter, having seen and experienced his share of racism within the department, said, "I hate to say this, 'cause I walked behind that shield for many a year, but I've walked in this skin for even longer. What you did was fail to observe Jim Crow etiquette. You didn't smile. You didn't say 'Yassuh' and 'Nawsuh.' And then you went on ahead and offended him by uttering a four-letter word: Yale. And as I stand here, I'm wondering what in the hell were you thinking with the search warrant bullshit? You coulda got you and your whole family killed tonight."

"Jim Crow? Really, Pop?!" Cedric said. "So, in 2016, I gotta smile when I ain't happy and scratch where I don't itch?!"

"I know what today's date is, son. But some things never change, I'm afraid. At least, they haven't yet."

Later that night, Marcus confided in Malcolm, "I won't lie. That cop still got me shook."

Malcolm, who still had steam coming out of his ears, didn't say much. He could think of nothing but naked revenge. But he poured his anger into a series of color-pencil sketches of the incident, including one that depicted a black family in a convertible luxury car. The family had been pulled over by the police. Though the police cruiser wasn't visible in the picture, the glow of flashing overhead lights illuminating the scene was unmistakable. Malcolm's attention to detail was most evident in the looks on the family members' faces: uncertainty for the kids, prayerfulness for the mom, and a boiling soup of rage, fear, and helplessness for the father in the driver's seat.

While Malcolm was pouring his rage into images, Marcus, who was also unable to sleep that night, made notes to himself about the cop who had tried to break his father down right in front of his, his brother's, and his mom's eyes. At one point,

Marcus wrote: He apparently missed his true calling as a neo-Nazi kook who goes to bible study at black churches then shoots the worshipers. Or maybe he's angry that he was born too late to be an overseer on a southern plantation with plenty of slaves to whip and treat like animals.

Marcus wouldn't have been able to forget the cop's face, even if he didn't have photographic memory. He wished he could draw as well as his brother. But Malcolm's sketches of the cop's big, yellow-toothed grin came close to the mental pictures that had begun to haunt Marcus's dreams and give him that plunging-on-a-rollercoaster feeling in the pit of his stomach in the instances that he'd seen the police since the incident.

Marcus couldn't stop thinking about how, after Cedric's breach of "Jim Crow etiquette," the officer went from zero to 100, real quick. The cop told Cedric, "If I have to ask you to get your ass out of that car again, I'm gonna drag you out and see if you can pass my own personal bar exam."

He'd pulled out his nightstick and was smacking it against the palm of his hand. "See what I did there," he said, "Bar? Exam?"

Seeing how quickly things had escalated, Cedric told Jaclyn to call his dad. Everybody heard Cedric say that, but as soon as she reached in the console to grab her phone, both of the cops drew their guns and the one standing on the passenger side put his gun right up against her temple.

"LET ME SEE YOUR HANDS! DON'T MOVE OR I'LL LIGHT YOU UP!"

Jaclyn said, as calmly as she could, with his pistol preventing her from turning her head to look at him, "Do you want to see my hands or do you want me to stay still?"

"GET 'EM UP! OR I SWEAR TO GOD..."

Marcus later told his grandfather, "The most scared I've ever been in my life was the moment I noticed that the cop's finger was on the trigger, and with her hands above her head, Mom was losing her grip on her cellphone. She was pinching it between her ring finger and the palm of her hand, but I could see it slowly sliding down. And I thought if that phone falls now, this might be the last time I ever see my mother alive.

So I started yelling,

'AYE, WHAT THE HELL, MAN! YOU KNOW WE HAVEN'T DONE ANYTHING—EXCEPT BE A LITTLE TOO DARK FOR YOUR TASTE. WHY DON'T YOU JUST COME TO WORK IN YOUR REAL UNIFORM? YOU KNOW, THE WHITE ONE WITH THE LITTLE POINTY HOOD.'

That did the trick."

The outburst, Marcus recalled, took the focus off of Jaclyn long enough for her to drop the phone in her lap without getting her head blown off.

"You know what the second-most-scary moment of my life was?" he said to his grandfather. "When he pointed his gun so I could see right down the barrel.

He hollered, 'HANDS UP! RIGHT NOW!' in that real jittery way that says he was about to squeeze off a bullet or some pee."

Marcus and Malcolm followed orders. That's when the cop on the driver's side proved himself to be a man of his word. He forced open the car door, dragged Cedric out onto the ground, rammed him in the gut with the end of the nightstick, then told him to roll over onto his stomach under threat of "getting a taste of lightning from this here taser."

He cuffed Cedric's wrists behind his back, dragged him up by his shackled hands, tossed him against the hood of the car, then kicked his legs apart so he'd be spread eagle.

Holding Cedric there in that position while he frisked him, the officer said, "Ain't got such a smart mouth now, huh, nigger? So, tell me, Mr. Yale University, what in the hell made you think you could come over to this side of town in your hoopty and drive back out to meet your homies in a sweet ride like this? Huh? Really, Yale? You couldn't just settle for a 3- or a 5-Series Bimmer. Noooo, not you. You had to have a 7-Series. I believe in giving the devil his due. And I gotta hand it to you, Yale. You've got a good eye for automobiles."

Marcus told his grandfather, "I already knew that Dad loved us. I did. But right then and there, it hit me, for the first time, how much his love for us is like God's love for us. With the side of his face up against that hot engine compartment and cars whizzing past the backs of his legs, he looked at us through the windshield and mouthed the words, 'It's okay.' And even though I was sitting there in the backseat with my hands above my head, tears streaming down my cheeks, and melted ice cream running down my arm, I felt a little better."

Jaclyn, who was listening to her son give his personal take on the seamy underbelly of law enforcement, began to cry as she recognized the parallel between that scene and the innumerable times before slavery was abolished that black men were publicly whipped, maimed, or lynched in order to instill terror in the hearts of their families and other enslaved Africans.

Her heart was breaking over the realization that 150 years after the Thirteenth Amendment (the one that was supposed to end slavery) was enacted, her sons had experienced the modern-day version of slave catchers randomly stopping black people and demanding to check their papers as if they were suspected of being runaways.

That's why they intentionally do a piss poor job of teaching history in school, Jaclyn thought. Wouldn't want us black people, who are supposed to believe that we've come so far, connecting old and new.

While the two cops were conducting their roadside "investigation," they never bothered to run Cedric's license or check the car's registration. They were too busy looking for the drugs they were sure they'd find in the vehicle or on the persons of the suspected car thieves. But Jaclyn was praying. Apparently, it worked.

Two more police cars raced up with their lights flashing just right about the moment the two cops pulled Jaclyn, Marcus, and Malcolm out of the car and made them sit on the ground with their hands bound with plastic zip ties.

A big, burly detective dressed in all black stepped out of a black, unmarked Dodge Charger. The cop who had assaulted Cedric greeted him.

Malcolm said he would never forget seeing just "how thirsty he was to impress" the detective. "He couldn't wait to show us off like we were on the auction block or something."

But the story took an even more dramatic turn when Cedric recognized the detective's voice. He stood up straight, trying to get his attention.

The officer who initiated the traffic stop turned, drew his gun, and yelled,

"GET DOWN OR I'LL LAY YOU DOWN!"

But the detective, after doing a double take and realizing who was standing two car lengths away, told the uniformed officer to stand down, then grabbed him by the front of his shirt and dragged him further away. Cedric, Jaclyn, and the twins could hear the detective yell at the uniformed cop as the two men stood by the trunk of the second squad car that had arrived on the scene after he and his partner radioed for backup.

Finally, without saying a word to any of the Carters, the uniformed cop walked up behind Cedric and unlocked the cuffs from his wrists.

He said, "Come on, Trent. Let's go. LET'S GO!" Then, as if none of what just happened had really happened, the two of them returned to their police cruiser, turned off the flashing overhead lights, pulled out into traffic, and slowly drove away into the fading daylight.

The detective, who had his gold police shield on a chain around his neck, walked over to Cedric and sighed because he was simply at a loss for words. He put his arm around Cedric and asked him to step over by the Dodge Charger.

Jaclyn, Marcus, and Malcolm were still shell shocked. It took the detective reassuring them twice that they could get back in the car before they even thought to get up off the ground. Then Malcolm raised his arms and showed the policeman that his fellow boys in blue hadn't bothered to remove the family's plastic restraints when they broke camp.

The detective shook his head in disgust. He and Cedric walked over to where the rest of the Carters were. Cedric stood off to the side while the detective snapped open a small hunting knife and carefully set them free.

"Imagine that. Our own personal 1865," Cedric said.

Jaclyn fell into her husband's arms and sobbed. But Malcolm was pissed.

"Is that it?!" he shouted. "They just get to drive away? Oh HELL no! I wanna see 'em get perp walked, mug shotted, fingerprinted... I wanna get a chance to draw courtroom sketches of their ugly, twisted faces for the nightly news. And nothing would make me happier—at least nothing legal— than knowing that they're on the inside with a gang of niggas, with no badge or gun to stand behind, and no backup on the way."

By that time Malcolm was wailing more than yelling,

"He coulda killed mommy and woulda sworn that he thought his life was in danger. Dad, you gotta make those... those..."

Cedric reassured him. "I know, son. I know. Trust and believe, in the fullness of time, those two will feel my wrath."

Normally, Cedric would have been annoyed at his son's use of the n-word. But in that moment, he couldn't argue with Malcolm's rage, and he felt in no position to police the boy's words. Cedric was angry himself. But he didn't have the capacity to deal with that emotion right then because he was still trying to recover from the nauseating feeling of helplessness in the pit of his stomach—right near the spot where the racist cop had struck him with the nightstick. That feeling had him asking himself, How can I chastise him for his word choice when I couldn't do anything to stop a white man from calling me a nigger to my face and, worse, treating me like one?

Cedric reached out and pulled Malcolm closer. "You all know that Clemens here is one of the good guys. I'm mad as hell and so is he. He's going to help me break those two idiots down to their very last compound. Then we'll see how they feel about their decision to hate black people more than they like feeding their families. So, know this, what happened here this evening won't be shifted behind the blue wall of silence the way we've seen with so many other police brutality cases.

And when they go back to the station to fill out that false report I know they're cooking up right now—trying to explain away their reckless and downright evil behavior out here on the side of this road—that paperwork will be the rope with which they hang themselves. And I wouldn't be me if I didn't kick the chair out from under their feet once they've put their necks in the noose."

Marcus's experience that night had scarred him. But just as importantly, it flipped a switch inside him that made him unafraid to speak truth to power. "Being quiet," he told his mom, "doesn't make you any safer than speaking up."

So, he felt no weight about sitting in the principal's office, across from his chemistry teacher, and reminding her that he thought she was hardly any better than the cops of whom she seemed to think so highly.

"Marcus... Mr. Carter... I'm sorry for what happened to you last weekend," Miss Orenstein said, putting on her instructor hat. "Marcus, I know you were scared, but the police have to do things sometimes that we don't necessarily understand. We might not think it's fair, but we don't then get to do whatever we want just because we're upset about the way things are going."

By that point, everyone else in the room was picking up what she was putting down. They—even Fortson—were wide-eyed with disbelief that she was choosing to frame the situation in a way that said the boy's anger was the result of his ignorance or childlike innocence. Marcus was about to interject, but Cedric put his hand on Marcus's leg—an unseen signal that he should let her continue without interruption.

"Look. Things worked out okay, didn't they?" she asked. "You were stopped. You were searched.

It was a bit of an inconvenience. But eventually, you were on your way, none the worse for wear.

You and your family may be good people. But I know that I, for one, feel safer knowing that the police are out there making stops like that. Who knows? The next car they stopped could've been full of druggies or hoodlums ready to walk into a convenience store and shoot up the place."

Cedric was content to let her continue giving Fortson an earful of what safety means to her. But Marcus could no longer contain himself.

"Exactly what I said! You couldn't care less whether I live or die! There's a price to pay for the safety you're so thirsty for. And people like me— and my dad, my mom, and my brother—keep getting handed the bill. Way too many of us are paying with our lives. And even when we don't get killed, we get beaten, harassed, and put through the system for no reason. Sometimes it's only because the person didn't do enough to keep all the hot air in some cop's inflated ego."

Cedric closed his eyes and began to nod in agreement as he took in just how well his son had absorbed the lessons from the previous weekend and the family's regular dinner-table discussions.

Marcus was on a roll.

"If we get burnt up on the altar of your personal comfort by a system set up to safeguard your white privilege above everything else, then... Well, so be it, right? But let the police start pulling over skinny blonde chicks, dragging them out of their cars, and slapping them around—as if that would ever happen—I can hear you right now, '*This is an outrage! I'm gonna write my congressman!*'"

"Now who's being racist?" Miss Orenstein said, more an accusation than a question. "We all know what would happen if I referred to either of you as a big black dude."

"Wait. What?" Marcus said. "I think we need to restate the definition of racism. Whether you wanna admit it or not, there's a racial caste system here in America, with white people at the top. The system is designed to create favorable outcomes for white people, regardless of the situation. So, even if what I said meant that I have racialized bias against you—which I don't—I don't have the power to negatively affect your life outcomes the way a white teacher can obviously do with a black student. And what's killin' me is how you still wanna tell yourself how good and liberal you are. Or should I say, how fair and balanced you are. I bet you stand in the mirror every morning and paraphrase a couple of lines from that movie *The Help*. You look at yourself and say, '*You is smart. You is kind. You is important. You is progressive.*'"

It was Cedric's turn to hold in a cackle.

"Okay, Marcus," Dr. Fortson said. "I think we get your point."

"I don't think you do. She comes in here every day and polishes up her sainthood street cred by working among 'those people.' That way, when she starts off a sentence with 'I'm not a racist, but...' she's already patted herself on the back and told herself that she's basically a moral person."

Miss Orenstein interrupted. "Huh! I've heard you're an inventive writer. But fiction is for books. And I don't need to hear about you imagining me in my bedroom."

"Don't do that," Marcus replied. "Whatever it is you call yourself doing right now, you're doing way too much."

"I'm just saying, you don't know what goes on in my head."

"Okay. You're right. But what's absolutely true is that you wanna make it okay when you say something foul. Case in point: Why would you tell me to put myself in the cops' shoes? Did it ever cross your mind that once the police know you think that way, they feel like they have your stamp of approval for anything they do—as long as they're not doing it to you? Or maybe you have thought about it, but you're cool with it. Must be nice, enjoying that privilege and not even knowing you have it."

"Alright, already! ENOUGH!" the chemistry teacher shouted. "Play the race card all you want, but I didn't come in here to get a history or a sociology lesson from either of you," she said. "Much as I feel for you and your family, Marcus, that doesn't excuse your behavior in my class— which is the real reason why we're here."

"What behavior?" Marcus asked. "You mean sitting there while you screamed in my face then tried to drag me up out of my seat? You're telling me there's no excuse for that?"

Fortson finally jumped back into the fray.

"According to Miss Orenstein, you lost control. She says you even went so far as to yank her arm after she asked you to leave the room."

"And as troubled as you might be right now," Orenstein added, "that's assault, so..."

Fortson finished the thought. "I'm afraid this falls under the district's zero-tolerance policy. Look, Marcus. You're obviously a good kid and a very bright student. I wish there were something I could do, but my hands are tied."

"In what sense?" Cedric asked.

"Assaulting a teacher calls for a mandatory suspension for a calendar year and demands that we report the matter directly to the police."

"Really?" Cedric replied. "So you're sitting here telling me that you're prepared to declare my son *persona non grata* for the final eight weeks of his sophomore year and the overwhelming majority of his junior year because she *claims* she was assaulted? I wish I could say I'm the least bit shocked at how cold-hearted and callous this whole setup is."

"Callous? Hmmph!" Miss Orenstein said in response to Cedric's assessment of the proposed punishment. "These rules are here for a reason, to provide the stick to kids who can't seem to respond to the carrot."

"As I was saying," Cedric continued, as though the teacher's comment were a pebble that had fallen into a bottomless well, "Institutions like this are part of a system that doesn't give a second thought about grinding black boys into powder. Whatever you say your intent is—and Miss Orenstein's is decidedly malicious—that's the outcome. And the outcome is what concerns me.

"Excuse you?" Orenstein said.

She turned to Fortson. "Are you gonna let him continue to talk down to me like this? Instead of focusing on his son's actions, he wants to make me the villain? The very idea of you sitting here listening to him trying to spin this and turn a sow's ear into a silk purse is an insult. Since we're being so blunt, open, and honest, and not concerned about people's feelings, I've got a bunch of test papers to grade and a mountain of other paperwork to get through, so we need to wrap this up."

Her eyes were locked on Fortson's. A small part of the reason for the sustained eye contact was her desire to rally the principal to act as her champion.

But it was mainly due to her inability to look Cedric in the eye while saying, in not so many words, that if the meeting was going to end up with Marcus ground into fine dust, they needed to get the crank turning so they could all move on with their day.

Orenstein couldn't have misjudged the principal's body language any worse than she did. The teacher thought her boss was in league with her and was indicating concern for her need to get her work done. But Fortson was horrified at the chemistry teacher's tone-deaf rant and her set-'em-up-and-knock-'em-down attitude.

"You're absolutely correct," Marcus's father said. Why delay the inevitable, right? So, let's talk about the procedural rules."

Turning to Fortson, he continued, "I've heard you talk about punishment, as if that were a done deal. But you've yet to drop even the first hint about due process."

Orenstein rolled her eyes, sat back in her chair and fumed. *There goes happy hour with the girls or any hope of getting to bed before midnight.*

Cedric continued. "As should be obvious from Marcus's permanent record, I've never had occasion to sit in on a school disciplinary hearing. So, let's go through the steps so I'll know exactly how to keep my son from being railroaded. And let's do it expeditiously. After all, Miss Orenstein's papers aren't going grade themselves."

The sarcasm wasn't lost on Fortson, but she didn't want to laugh for fear of making it obvious that she'd begun to take Marcus's side.

"Well, since we don't have a court stenographer, we need to make an official record of what we say from this point forward. I'm going to tape record what'll be Miss Orenstein's and Marcus's official statements. Miss Orenstein, please start with your full name and your position, then tell us everything you remember about the incident."

"Abigail Orenstein. Science teacher, Hamilton East High School. I'm committed to my students. I work hard to make science fun and accessible…"

Marcus could certainly co-sign those first few statements. Her chemistry class *was* fun, he thought. She was actually a good teacher.

She continued. "So, today, I was teaching my AP chemistry class. We've been discussing the properties of chemicals, and I wanted to do something a little different.

I started the class by passing around a big bag of gummy bears. The kids, being kids, were certainly up for that. Before long, I asked them, 'What if I told you that you just ate one of the ingredients in a reaction that, if packaged right, could cause a really big boom?'

For a second, the room was dead silent. I knew I had 'em. Eyes in front. Full attention.

I told them that if we added enough energy in the form of heat, we could get the gummy bear to react with a compound called potassium chlorate. I turned on the Bunsen burner under a glass test tube containing some potassium chlorate powder, and after about a minute or so, the flame had turned the powder into a liquid. I removed the burner, turned off the overhead lights, then dropped in one gummy bear.

Nothing but oohs and ahhs and jaws dropping.

The violent decomposition reaction between the sugar in the gummy bear and oxygen given off by the potassium chlorate when we heated it up gave off a lot of heat, a lot of light, but most importantly—at least in terms of an explosion—a lot of gas. I explained that because the top end of the test tube was open and the gas was able to escape without the pressure building up inside the vessel, no big deal. But I asked them to imagine what would happen if: 1) we added a lot more than the couple of spoonfuls of potassium chlorate we used in our experiment (and, of course, a lot more gummy bears); and 2) we started the reaction inside a sealed container that didn't allow the gas to escape.

When I was designing the lesson, I imagined that that bit of theatrics would be the springboard into a longer discussion of how, with just a little nudging, inert—or even edible—substances can release a shocking amount of energy. But things went south when Marcus said he needed to learn to make bombs so he could go out and kill police."

Marcus angrily interrupted her. "I told you that wasn't me! And that's not what he said, anyway."

Fortson cautioned him to remain quiet while the teacher was giving her statement.

"Well, tell her to stop making stuff up! Fiction is for books, remember?"

"Don't worry, Marcus," the principal assured him. "You'll have ample opportunity to tell your side of the story as soon as she's done. Okay?"

"Yeah, whatever." *Y'all better put some respeck on my name*, he thought.

"Go ahead, Miss Orenstein," Fortson said.

"I couldn't believe my ears. I mean, what kind of evil mind would think of going out and killing police officers? He should have quit while he was behind, but he tried to justify doing something that horrendous by dragging up the death of the boy in Cleveland... What's his name? ...Umm—"

"Tamir Rice," Cedric said.

"Yeah. It's sad that he died, but no matter what you think about it, you can't possibly think it's okay to stage an attack on the police. I was offended. Okay, I'll admit it. I was angry. And I told him as much. But he wouldn't let it go. So, you know what? I told him to take himself and his cop-murder fantasies and get out of my classroom. Not only did he refuse to leave, but he grabbed my arm and yanked it, sending me sprawling over the furniture. That's when I sent a note to the office asking for Mr. Grodski to handle it.

For the record, Marcus is a good student. But I can't have him back in my class. Not now. I'm here to teach, not fight."

Before Fortson could press the stop button on her antiquated mini-cassette machine, there was a knock at the office door.

Millie the secretary stuck her head in and announced, "Dr. Fortson, you have a, um, 'special guest.' Should I send him in?"

For a moment, Fortson was paralyzed. But she finally responded, telling Millie to give them a few more minutes.

"Who is your special guest?" Cedric asked. "And if they have anything to do with this, I'd like to hear what they have to say."

Cedric wasn't a betting man, but if asked, he would have wagered a year's salary on the identity of the person waiting in the main office. He was sure that it was his own mystery guest—the person he'd called before Fortson returned from her meeting at the district office. But the principal and the teacher had no way of knowing that.

"What's wrong, Dr. Fortson?" Cedric asked. "No, wait. Let me guess. It's part two of your zero-tolerance policy. Which means that the end of this story was written not long after it began."

"Well, uh, we… That's not it at all," Fortson stammered. "The protocol—"

"Let me help you out," Cedric offered. "The words you're looking for are: The protocol for the school-to-prison pipeline calls for the police to take over, regardless of what evidence is presented. Or, in this case, whether any is presented at all. But please, by all means, call in your special guest."

"We haven't gotten Marcus's statement yet." Fortson said. "Perhaps we should…"

"No. I'd hate to keep Officer Part Two waiting. And let's not forget Miss Orenstein's all-important paperwork."

"Wait!" Marcus said. "Dr. Fortson, can I say something?" he asked.

"Yes, Marcus. Of course."

"The zero-tolerance policy is what it is. But it doesn't apply to this situation. I didn't do what she's saying I did. So, just know. You have a choice. You can go along with her in making this into something it isn't or you can shut it down. Don't do this to me.

It's like I'm not supposed to remember how you treat other people. I was there in the lunchroom a few weeks ago when two white boys, Travis and Austin, were fighting and Mr. Sweet got hurt trying to break it up. They got suspended for a week, but they came right back, like nothing happened. But me? You're ready to give me the death penalty and nothing even happened to her. So, this is a Bill Klem situation."

"A what?" Dr. Fortson asked.

"Bill Klem. My grandfather was telling me about him the other week. He was a baseball umpire back in the day. He's mostly remembered for telling a batter who was arguing over whether a pitch was a ball or a strike, 'It ain't nothin' til I call it.' Well, this is a Bill Klem situation. It ain't nothin' til you call it."

Fortson's blood pressure was peaking, as she thought about whether the point Marcus was making was true. *Am I reinforcing white privilege? Can I stop this ball from rolling—especially now that the police are already here?*

Regardless of the outcome, Fortson knew that having jumped the gun on calling the police could give Mr. Carter grounds to appeal any decision to punish Marcus. But she couldn't press the backspace key on the officer's arrival and on Millie looking to unwrap the gift of seeing Carter watch helplessly as his son was dragged off in handcuffs.

I hate this part of my job, she thought. *This is not what I came here for. This is not why I became a teacher in the first place.* She could feel a tension headache coming on.

The principal reluctantly opened the door and beckoned the policeman to enter. The plain-clothes cop had just pulled rank, assuring the uniformed officer who'd been dispatched after Dr. Fortson's phone call that he would handle things from that point on. Despite expectations, everyone seated at the table was happy to see him.

Orenstein envisioned herself climbing the tower of muscle and upon reaching the summit, setting up camp. But before that, he'd do her the favor of getting rid of the nuisance who'd hijacked her class discussion and followed that up by ruining her plans for the evening.

Marcus looked at Cedric in stunned silence.

The detective, who was dressed in black fatigues, black military-style boots, and a long sleeved black t-shirt, with his gold police shield hung from a chain around his neck, shook Fortson's hand and introduced himself, "Detective Sergeant Clemens. How's it goin'?"

"Pleasure to meet you, Sgt. Clemens. I'm Dr. Fortson, the principal. This is Mr. Carter and his son, Marcus. And this is Miss Orenstein, Marcus's chemistry teacher. She's accused Marcus of assaulting her, so we've got a serious situation on our hands."

"Hey, Cedric." the detective said.

"What's up, Clem?"

"You two know each other?" Fortson asked.

"Very well, I'd say," the officer replied as he went over to shake hands with Cedric and Marcus, then turned to greet Miss Orenstein.

"What's it been, Cedric? Sixteen, seventeen years since we first met?"

He turned to face Fortson and continued his short trip down memory lane.

"He was a rookie prosecutor and I was fresh out of the academy. Now look at him. Just named number two at the DA's office. I felt honored, testifying in a big court case he was heading up a few weeks back. We put away a big-time druglord. You should see this guy in front of a jury. I imagine it's like watching van Gogh standing in front of a canvas."

Because of his position as a prosecutor, Cedric had frequently witnessed the fallout from uniformed police showing up in the middle of situations like this. They'd hear the words *hit, assault,* or *attack* thrown around and place a kid under arrest without the slightest bit of physical evidence. He'd personally dismissed his share of cases where the cops were overzealous to make an arrest but the evidence was so thin that there was plenty of reasonable doubt.

When you're programmed to make cans, eventually you come to see everything as can-making material, was Cedric's philosophy on why so many black and brown kids were getting swept into the criminal justice system. And, he didn't want Marcus to be mistaken for a piece of aluminum. So, he'd pulled a card that most parents in that situation don't have up their sleeves. He called Clemens, the detective who had saved the day the previous Saturday when the Carter family came perilously close to being hashtags like #philandocastile, #ericgarner, and #tamirrice.

Orenstein was suddenly less attracted to the police officer.

Doesn't matter, she told herself. *He could be Carter's next-door neighbor or his best friend for all I care. At the end of the day, G.I. Joe is taking that smart-mouthed, pain-in-the-ass kid off to jail—and out of my hair.*

Fortson removed her eyeglasses and pinched the bridge of her nose. *This can't be happening,* she said to herself. *The lead criminal prosecutor? His buddy on the force?*

The principal tried to regain control of the situation by directing traffic. "So, uh, Sgt. Clemens. We were just about to get young Mr. Carter's statement about what happened. If you could—"

"Hold up a second," the policeman demanded. "You're still trying to figure out what happened?"

"There's nothing to figure out." Orenstein shouted. "We all KNOW what happened. Right, Marcus? I think you'd better go ahead and 'fess up or it's only going to be worse for you."

"Wowwwww…" was all Marcus could say in response to her badgering. But he didn't need to say anything more.

"To answer your question," Cedric said to the detective, "You're here because this mean-spirited, morally-corrupt person has every intention of pressing the eject button on my son. Her plan, so far as I've been able to ascertain, is to make her accusation—with no witness statements to back her up—a smoking gun. You already know what the next steps in the plan are: chucking him from the school system and right onto the conveyor belt to feed him into the school-to-prison pipeline."

Cedric turned his attention to Orenstein. "You know that most kids who get suspended after the tenth grade never finish school, right? But not this kid. Not on my watch."

"Because your buddy here is gonna try to sweep this whole thing under the rug, right?" Orenstein hissed. "Typical."

Just then, Marcus's phone pinged.

"Turn off your phone, son," an annoyed Cedric said. "Does this look like the time to be playing with one of your apps? In case you haven't figured it out, your life is on the line here. And I, for one, am scared to death of what could happen to you if Miss 'I Need to Grade My Papers' gets her way."

Marcus leaned in and whispered in his father's ear. "No, Dad. You gotta see this. Somebody sent me a video."

Before Marcus could press play, Cedric did a double take. The person who'd posted the two-and-a-half-minute clip from the chemistry class labeled it, "Racist AF Teacher Goes Worldstar."

"Is this...?" Cedric asked Marcus.

"Yup."

"Send your mother and me a copy right now."

Cedric bowed his head. *God, I thank you for being faithful. You always come through.*

After acknowledging the Almighty for working in mysterious ways, he took a deep breath before flashing the wide smile that you wear only when you're assured of victory.

"Miss Orenstein," he said, "I'd like to thank you SO MUCH for being so predictable, so arrogant... so foolish. I'd also like to enter into the record Marcus's written statement about the classroom incident and this video that, I believe, actually supports every word of his account."

"YOU RECORDED ME?" she screamed at Marcus. "You little—"

Cedric slapped the table. Hard.

"Watch yourself," he warned.

Orenstein's switch from aggressor back to self-proclaimed victim was instantaneous. "I've never, in my entire life, been treated this way," she said, her eyes starting to water.

No one in the room missed the cues she was giving with her body language as she slid her chair back from the table and clasped her open shirt collar in her tiny fist to close it. "These threats and intimidation…" she said, lowering her head to make it seem as though the fight had been beaten out of her.

I can smell her scent, Cedric thought. *But White Fragility isn't a fragrance I happen to like.*

"Maybe I need a lawyer," Orenstein said.

"Ya think?" Cedric replied.

"Why didn't you tell us you had a video?" Fortson asked Marcus.

"'Cause I didn't have it. Well, not until just now."

"But it came not a moment too soon," Cedric said. "It gave us a chance to see the lengths to which she'd go to punish Marcus for speaking a truth that contradicts the lie she lives. And she unspooled the entire tape measure, didn't she? So, since we're all here, and she's already made her official statement, why don't we check out the video?"

Sgt. Clemens, who'd parked his six-foot-four-inch frame on the window ledge behind Orenstein rather than sitting at the table, got up and stood behind the chair separating the teacher and the principal.

Cedric motioned for Marcus to slide his phone across the table.

"B-b-but you can't do this!" Orenstein pleaded. "That's completely out of context. I didn't give my permission to be recorded. This is an invasion of privacy."

The instant she realized that Fortson was more interested in seeing exactly what was on that video file than listening to any more of her muddled Fourth Amendment privacy argument, she grabbed Marcus's phone, raised it above her head, and slammed it onto the polished concrete floor.

"MISS ORENSTEIN!" the principal shouted.

Marcus was out of his chair the instant he heard the crunch that told him she'd done major damage.

"Yo, you wildin' out. I just got that phone." he screamed as he raced over to pick up the damaged electronic device and see whether it still worked. Marcus, from his knees, held the phone in the air so the others could see the shattered screen.

Cedric gave voice to everyone's thoughts. "If I weren't here, witnessing this firsthand, I'd never believe it. I'd say, 'She couldn't possibly be that stupid.' But I'm here. And you are."

"Listen, I'm sick of your name calling—"

"Stop! Enough!" Fortson shouted. She felt like the meeting had gone off the rails, and she had reached the end of her patience with the bickering.

After a moment of awkward silence, Cedric said, "I have a copy of the video on my phone. So does his mother. And so do half of the students at this school, I'm guessing."

Orenstein didn't hear Cedric when he made the declarative statement that she was going to replace Marcus's phone by the end of the week. A trail of tears had begun running down her right cheek. Behind her vacant, thousand-yard stare, she was flashing back to fifth period, to what her boss and the cop standing over her left shoulder were about to see.

"Miss Orenstein!" Fortson shouted. "Did you hear Mr. Carter?"

That was enough to momentarily bring her forward in time and out of her head.

"Uh-huh," she said, between sniffles.

"Marcus, please give me the details about what kind of phone that is. Miss Orenstein will replace it by week's end.

"How much is that thing?" she said, concerned about the impact the purchase would have on her wallet.

"I suspect, the same as it was before you committed that act of vandalism," Sergeant Clemens said.

Cedric reached in his inside jacket pocket, pulled out his iPhone 6, punched in his four-digit code, and made an important announcement,

"This phone had better not end up on the floor, or we'll definitely see if those metal bracelets on Sgt. Clemens' belt match your outfit."

Clemens leaned over and retrieved the phone, then gently placed it on the table so that he and Fortson both had a good viewing angle.

The instant the policeman pressed play, the principal's office was filled with the sound of Orenstein's angry shrieks.

"You know what?! I'm sick of this! Get out of my room!"

They were also met with Marcus's attempts to get the train back on the rails.

"All I said was—" and *"That wasn't me."*

Fortson and Clemens were both caught off guard when fifth-period Orenstein said, *"I heard what you said, goddammit! Now tell your story walking!"*

And just as Marcus had described it in his written statement, Orenstein damn near vaulted from her position at the front of the room to the spot in the back row where Marcus liked to sit because it gave him the best vantage point for studying his classmates' mannerisms for later use in his writing.

Fortson had shifted forward in her seat to get closer to the phone's screen. She could sense that the moment that would determine whether she'd be expelling one of her best students or firing one of her best teachers was fast approaching.

Orenstein, who was present for the making of the video and well aware of the performance she had turned in, sat silently rocking back and forth.

Then it happened.

Orenstein grabbed Marcus's forearm in a comically inept attempt to pull him out of his seat. After her second tug, Marcus snatched his arm away, sending her sprawling over the L-shaped writing surface of his chair-desk combo and knocking his three-ring binder onto the floor.

Dr. Fortson and Sgt. Clemens, now fully caught up on the 180-degree difference between the statement recorded on Fortson's mini-cassette and what they'd just seen on the video, both looked to Orenstein for an explanation. But, by that point, there was also a 180-degree difference between the posture of the enraged, "my way or the highway" teacher seen in the video, and the one who sat in the heavy wooden chair in the principal's office with her watery eyes closed, arms folded, and her back hunched.

Fortson took a deep breath and exhaled slowly in a way that puffed out her cheeks. Then she straightened up in her chair and spoke:

"Mr. Carter, I sincerely apologize. I wish—"

Cedric put up his hand and interrupted her.

"Before you get too far gone with your apology, let me just say that you're addressing the wrong Mr. Carter. I'm not the one who was lied on. I'm not the one who, because of that lie, was on the brink of being denied a high school education and stamped with the life-altering label "CRIMINAL." So, you might want to readjust your focus."

Cedric managed to fight off the urge to say, "The prosecution rests."

Fortson ran her long, slender fingers through her thick mane of chestnut brown hair, placed both of her palms on the tabletop to steady herself, and started again.

"Marcus."

"Marcus?"

The principal swallowed hard when she noticed the boy wasn't paying her the least bit of attention. His gaze and the burning rage it was transmitting were laser focused on the woman seated across the table from him.

Marcus was silently going off on her.

Hold on, he thought. *You were just going hard body tryna get me locked up for arguing while black. Now that you're staring up from the bottom of the hole you dug for me, you sittin' there acting like you made of cotton candy. But them fake-ass tears won't help you.*

Orenstein opened her eyes in order to find out just what was behind the sudden silence. When she saw Marcus's icy glare and noticed his tightened fists sitting on the tabletop like two hammers, she shuddered.

Cedric nudged his son.

"I can hear you, Dr. Fortson," said the boy. But he refused to break eye contact with Orenstein. He wasn't finished writing an open letter with his body language that was addressed to the science teacher.

Fortson, aware that half of Marcus's attention was the best she could expect, forged ahead.

"Listen, Marcus. I... I'm truly sorry for putting you through all this. You're obviously a great kid. And, well... I know you might not believe it, but it pained me to have to carry out the district policy. I just... Like I said, it doesn't leave much wiggle room in cases like this. I hope you understand."

Marcus finally shifted his gaze to Fortson, but didn't move his head or the rest of his body.

"Keep your apology," he said to the principal. "We both know it would've been a wrap for me if somebody didn't record her buggin' out in the middle of class. You're all in your feelings now, but five minutes ago, you were on some 'She said it, I believe it, and that settles it.' So, all I really wanna hear about right now is when *her* zero-tolerance policy is gonna kick in."

"He makes a good point," Cedric said.

"Well... I can't just... There are procedures—"

"I know," Marcus said. "Your hands are tied."

"Well, mine aren't," Cedric said. "I'm getting up early in the morning. I'm gonna get dressed in a hurry and skip breakfast. I won't even stop for coffee. And the very first thing I'm going to do when I get to work at the crack of dawn is direct one of the prosecutors in my office to file assault charges."

"Is that really necessary, Mr. Carter?" Fortson asked Marcus's dad.

"Oh yes. Like the school district, the state has its own zero-tolerance policy. And because I'm an officer of the court, it leaves me little in the way of discretion. I'm sure you understand."

That wasn't exactly true, but Cedric had no intention of letting Orenstein off the hook, and he relished throwing Fortson's words back at her.

"So, what are we looking at?" the principal asked.

"Well, a teacher accused of assaulting a student must be immediately removed from the classroom pending an investigation—which isn't an issue short term, since she'll go into the system this evening and won't be in court for arraignment until after the start of school in the morning."

Cedric realized that he was getting ahead of himself. He added, "But I defer to Sgt. Clemens with regard to what happens right this instant."

The police officer took a step back and pulled the handcuffs from his belt.

"Wait. What are you doing?" Orenstein asked. Pure terror over the prospect of being led away from the school with her hands cuffed behind her back was written on her tear-soaked and makeup-stained face.

"That wasn't assault," she argued. "You saw it yourself. He refused to leave. He refused to... I was just trying to get him to leave."

Listen at her, coppin' pleas now, Marcus said to himself. *Excuses much?*

"Look. There's gotta be some way we can work this out," Orenstein pleaded. "Dr. Fortson?"

"What do you expect me to do?" she asked. "I mean, really. Mr. Carter and Sgt. Clemens wouldn't even be here if you hadn't decided that you were going to show Marcus who's boss once and for all. And for what? I can't even imagine what would make you do something so mean-spirited."

Bruh! What part of she's a racist bitch are you not seeing? Marcus thought. *Like I've been saying this whole time: To her, black lives really don't matter.*

"Not only was it mean-spirited AND abusive of the system," Cedric said, "it would have been irreversible."

Looking Orenstein directly in the eye, he said, "If Marcus had been kicked out of school this close to finals, how could you undo him failing all of the classes he's taking now? If he spent one day in jail, what power do you have to give that day back? And after his wrongful arrest, what institutional authority would you have brought to bear to get his fingerprints and mugshots removed from the police database so he's not listed among the ranks of actual criminals?"

"I'm sorry. I'm soooo sorry," she pleaded as Clemens helped her to her feet and closed one of the cuffs on her wrist. She started to go limp like a ragdoll, but Clemens held her up. "Don't do this," she begged. "I can't go to jail. It's just me and my daughter. I'm all she has."

"So, you figured you'd support your daughter by getting this man's son expelled and put behind bars?" Fortson asked.

"I didn't mean it like that."

"Like what? Cedric wondered. "You didn't mean to institutionalize your racism?"

"You're mixing up my words. This is so not right."

"Not right, huh?" Marcus replied. He turned to Sgt. Clemens and said, "Come on. Let's get with the 'You have the right to remain silent' part."

"Dr. Fortson, do something! Please." Orenstein demanded as the detective pulled her free arm behind her back so he could close the other cuff around that wrist.

The detective read the teacher her rights, and then guided her to the office door.

"BYE, FELICIA," said Marcus.

Cedric glared at him. "This is no time to be smug, son. You were this close to being in those handcuffs yourself. If I were you, I'd be thanking

God right now for just how different this outcome was from what too many black boys experience."

Still, before Fortson closed the door, Marcus called out to the teacher, "Miss Orenstein, BLACK LIVES MATTER!"

Cedric gave Marcus a hard jab with his elbow. Then he admonished him, "What part of 'Don't be a sore winner' did you fail to understand?"

*****

That evening, Cedric, Marcus, and Malcolm sat at the dinner table. Marcus could hardly eat because he was so focused on recounting for Malcolm every detail of what happened after he'd left the school and went to work.

"Real talk, Dad," Malcolm said during a lull in his brother's story. "Why do white people play so many games?"

"Because they can," Marcus replied.

Cedric put down his fork and considered how he wanted to respond.

Racism is a sickness, he thought. Then he decided to go another way.

"Well, think about it," he told the boys. "What if you found yourself in a system that's set up to make you right, even when you're wrong; proclaim that you're good, even when your actions are evil by any objective measure; call you pure and beautiful and honest and upright, even when you're none of those things? I think you might find it hard not to take advantage of that system from time to time. There's power in it. And power corrupts."

"Yeah. Like those two racist cops who stopped us on Saturday night," Malcolm said.

"Exactly," his dad replied. "Rotten to the core. But instead of it being another data point proving that black people are viewed as the prime targets of the system, it gets explained away—"

"They're just two bad apples, huh?" Marcus interjected.

"Isolated incident," said Malcolm.

"There you go," said Cedric. "There's a reason why some people, for the life of them, can't believe that the way police treat black and brown people is part of a larger program. Back to my analogy: If you're born into this system, you and the other people who benefit from it are going to do whatever you can to keep it going. One of those things just happens to be acting like it doesn't exist. They can't admit it."

"Shoot. Miss Orenstein won't even admit she lied on Marcus."

"Even right now, sitting down at the police station with Clemens, I'll bet in her mind, she's still making Marcus and me the bad guys in her story. And what did we do to her? Your brother checked her on that ridiculous, Fox News analysis of what police should be able to get away with. I came in and challenged her claim that he assaulted her. We got lucky and had proof dropped in our laps. But the fact that there are evil wretches like your science teacher in this world is not the lesson you should be taking away from this crazy week."

"Then what is it?" Malcolm asked.

"You tell me," his father said.

Marcus thought about it for a moment, and then responded. "Honestly, I don't think there's a lesson,

Dad. I mean, aren't lessons supposed to change the way you think or the way you act? What should I have done to keep from being the latest black male accused of hurting a poor lil' white woman? And I've already asked myself a thousand times what we could have done differently when we got pulled over the other night. I got nothin'. I don't know. Really, I'm asking. What lesson am I supposed to have learned from that?"

"Duck when they're shooting," Malcolm said. "And keep quiet when they're telling you it's your fault you didn't duck fast enough."

All three of the Carter men laughed the kind of laugh that keeps you from crying.

"And we know what you're gonna say, Dad," Marcus added. "We can't put that on all white people. But I don't need to learn that lesson. I already knew that."

Cedric finished what remained in his wine glass and poured himself some more. *Damn, I wish Jackie were here right now*, he said to himself. *She always knows how to paint a picture—even without a brush or a pencil in her hand.*

"I know," Cedric said. "It's easy to think that nothing good can come from this. But this incident has forced me to take a hard look at how I wield the power of my office. I mean, how should you use whatever power, whatever advantages you have in life?"

Looking at Marcus, he said, "Miss Orenstein decided to use her power to try to destroy you. But I'm going another way. I'm toying with an idea. By this time tomorrow, your chemistry teacher will be lawyered up. And I know, as sure as I'm sitting here, that her attorney will come at me looking to hammer out some sort of deal. And here's my bottom line, take-it-or-leave-it offer.

In exchange for a pre-trial diversion—"

"What's that?" Malcolm asked.

"Basically, a prosecutor, with the approval of a judge, can set aside the charges against a criminal defendant as long as they agree to meet certain conditions. Usually, it's completing a certain number of hours of community service and upholding their promise to stay out of trouble. In Miss Orenstein's case, that will let her avoid having to sit through a criminal trial and give her at least a crackhead-thin chance of remaining a licensed teacher."

"Wait. What?!" a shocked Marcus shouted. "She was ready to send me to prison. And I'm supposed to be cool with you giving her ZERO jail time? Community service? Really, Dad?"

"Marcus. I feel you. Still, you oughta know me well enough by now to know that I've got something real good planned for her.

I'm gonna keep it real with you guys. Right now, I'm pissed to the height of pisstivity. But remember what I just said about the use of power. I'd be a horrible parent if I taught you that it's okay to go for payback over anything else, just because you're angry. You need to see power handled wisely instead of the way a petulant child would. So, although I'd love to get revenge on your science teacher—and I easily could—what I want more than that is to make sure the teachers, administrators, and staff at your school become aware of their implicit bias—the prejudices they hold that they don't even recognize.

Now, I could push for Miss Orenstein to be sent off to jail and not give her another thought. But the story would end there, and that's not what you do with power. At least, that's not what you're supposed to do."

"So, what *are* you doing?" Malcolm asked.

"I'm thinking bigger than seeing her in an orange jumpsuit, even though that's exactly what she had in mind for your brother.

I'd prefer that you two—and all the black and brown kids who'll walk the halls of Hamilton East after you're long gone—be in the hands of people who recognize that they have to unlearn negative attitudes about black people. I want them—even the black teachers—actively working on recognizing when they're viewing black boys and girls the way TV, movies, and newspapers have programmed us all to see them.

That's the hard part. There are plenty of people who don't even mean to be biased. They want to do the right thing. But they have a hard time overcoming years of subtle training telling them that white is good and black is bad, even when it doesn't line up with their conscious opinions.

Notice I said the black teachers too. Quiet as it's kept, black people are also susceptible to that ugly, demeaning way of thinking, if we don't actively fight against it.

But I'm thinking, maybe if people know better, perhaps they'll do better. And that's what I'm concerned with...better outcomes."

"So, what does any of this have to do with you deciding not to prosecute Miss Orenstein?" Malcolm asked.

Cedric laughed. *That boy's never had a latch on his tongue*, he thought. Then he shared the plan he'd begun hatching the instant Sgt. Clemens drove off with the science teacher in the back of his unmarked vehicle.

"Whether she knows it or not, Miss Orenstein's going to be an agent for change. She's going to participate in the very next "Undoing Racism" workshop offered by The People's Institute for Survival and Beyond.

And she won't just sit there like a bump on a log, either. She's going to put her all into every one of the activities they do—the reflections, the role-playing, the presentations, even the strategic planning. It's in her best interest that she come away with not only an understanding of what racism actually is and what forms it takes, but also a good sense of the what's, why's, and how's of systemic racism. She'd better know how these institutions came to be, who they're designed to serve, and the impact of that design. And Lord knows, she'd better pay attention when they start focusing on how to build multiracial coalitions as a way to start undoing racism."

Malcolm hit his father with his most serious side eye. "And what's the point, other than making her miserable? You think they got some kind of magical red, black, and green wand they're gonna wave over her so she'll—bippity, boppity, boo—turn into a community organizer?"

"No, there'll be no magic wand. But yes, she'll become a community organizer. Her life depends on it. After Clemens hauled her off to get her police station glamour shots and fingerprinting done, Dr. Fortson asked me what I wanted to see happen at this point. Long story short: She's in full support of the second part of the terms I'm going to impose on Miss Orenstein.

In order to get back in the community's good graces, her mission—should she choose to accept it—will be to organize an annual community anti-racism event at your school. And she's gonna work with Dr. Fortson to design a set of school policies that help prevent black and Latino kids from being several times more likely to be suspended than their white classmates for the same types of infractions."

"And what makes you think she'll go through with it?" Malcolm asked.

"She might have the urge to resist—at least at first. She might have voices in her ear telling her that I'm violating her rights. But I'm gonna let her know right off the top that when she starts to feel some pushback—from her people or from inside her own head—she should remember the words of Galatians chapter 6, verse 9: '*And let us not be weary in well doing, for in due season we shall reap, if we faint not.*'

And if that doesn't help, she can look to the Book of Cedric, chapter 2, verse 1: '*Don't try to play me; for if thou mess with the bull, thou shalt get the horns.*'"

Malcolm and Marcus laughed.

"This oughta be good," Malcolm said. "I can't wait to see how it turns out."

Marcus raised his glass and toasted to his chemistry teacher's continuing education. "I guess she *is* gonna learn her lesson."

REAL TALK

Black people are victims of an enormous amount of violence… None of those things can take place without the complicity of the people who run the schools and the city.
—Toni Morrison

In a number of ways, Marcus's story is the exception that proves the rule. For far too many black boys who get in trouble at school, there isn't a happy ending. While it's understandable that a serious breach of school rules, like possessing a deadly weapon, merits a serious response, these days, seemingly everything rises to a level that supposedly demands that a student be ejected from school and cut off from the community of learning. Talking back to the teacher and a multitude of other discretionary offenses can very easily result in a child being pushed out of school for several days at a time.

Why? There's apparently been a shift in thinking, from an assumption that a teacher with sufficient classroom management skill should be able to quell most disruptions and handle problems without outside assistance, to a mode that devalues classroom management skill in favor of calling in the cavalry to toss away the children who are considered bad apples.[1] Worse, that shift has been accompanied by two other troubling phenomena. Children are being pushed out of school as a means of punishment at ever younger ages. Meanwhile, schools are becoming increasingly reliant on actual police officers (euphemistically referred to as "school resource officers" or "school safety officers") to maintain order and discipline. The shocking result: Six-year-olds are being handcuffed and detained for misbehaving.

If Marcus's fictional high school had employed a school resource officer, the boy would likely have been dragged away from the building long before his father had the chance to arrive on the scene and lend emotional and legal support. Sure, the video would have eventually proven that Marcus was not guilty of the charge leveled against him by Miss Orenstein. But that would have come too late to prevent him from being handcuffed and paraded in front of his teachers and peers, placed in the back of a police cruiser, taken to a police station, fingerprinted, photographed, and detained in a holding cell. There is nothing I'm aware of that could erase those experiences from Marcus's memory and blunt their traumatic effect on his psyche.

The changes in how schools maintain discipline and mete out punishment sit atop the racial fault line created when the ultra-punitive thinking behind states' minimum sentencing laws (including the so-called Three Strikes laws that created legions of lifetime enrollees in the prison industrial complex) struck hard against school districts' desire to find a way to turn back the tide of violence on school property.

When President Bill Clinton signed the Gun-Free Schools Act into law in 1994, schools that received federal funding were suddenly required to expel, for at least a year, any student who brought a firearm onto school premises.[2] It wasn't long before states got in on the act. The same legislatures that had prescribed mandatory minimum prison sentences for adults began applying this same thinking to schoolchildren. Their stated rationale: By getting the troublemakers out, the classroom can be made safe for kids who are serious about learning. The resulting zero-tolerance policies were supposedly color blind—if you do X, then Y is the consequence, and nothing else matters—but it hasn't worked out that way in practice.

Take for instance New York City, home to

America's largest public school system. Today, 27 percent of public school students in the five boroughs are black. It stands to reason that the portion of suspensions and expulsions handed down to black kids would be somewhere near that figure. But during the 2014–2015 school year, roughly 50 percent of the children who were suspended were black.[3] For New York City's white students, the picture is completely different. During that same school year, white children, who comprise about 15 percent of the city's student population, got 8 percent of the suspensions.[4]

Over the past decade, school resource officers in Bryan, Texas, got into the habit of issuing "Class C" criminal misdemeanor tickets for the kind of school-based behavior that school administrators previously handled. The majority of these tickets were for "Disruption of Class" or "Disorderly Conduct-Language."[5]

Though black children comprise less than 25 percent of the students in the Bryan Independent School District, there was a three-year stretch (2009–2012) during which they received more than half of all tickets issued. The fact that black children in Bryan were four times as likely as white kids in the district to receive one of these tickets for "Disruption of Class" or "Disorderly Conduct-Language" eventually drew the attention of the NAACP Legal Defense and Educational Fund and the National Center for Youth Law. When the two social justice groups filed a civil rights complaint with the U.S. Department of Education's Office for Civil Rights, and the office announced that it was opening an investigation into the disparity, the school district quickly moved to overhaul its discipline policy.[6]

Lest anyone think these examples—children victimized by a pattern of discriminatory behavior in big, bustling New York City and comparatively tiny Bryan, Texas—were isolated cases, they weren't. According to a U.S. Department of Education report on school discipline released in March 2014, black students nationwide are suspended and expelled at three times the rate of white students.[7]

So, are we observers expected to believe that white children are, by and large, better behaved than their black counterparts? The headline of a *Daily Beast* article published the same day the Department of Education report was released posed the question this way: "Are Black Students Unruly? Or is America Just Racist?"[8] (The author begins answering these questions by immediately recounting the true story of a black kindergartner being handcuffed, arrested, and charged with simple battery and criminal damage to property as punishment for having thrown a temper tantrum in class and in the principal's office.)

A broad array of researchers have presented a growing body of empirical evidence showing that black youth aren't more violent or more likely to engage in other criminal behavior than white juveniles. But as with most every other aspect of American society, school policies have been built on a framework that leaves black Americans over-policed and under-protected.[9]

Researchers have written quite a bit about the disproportionality of black youth being arrested, detained, and jailed in comparison with their numbers in the overall population. But most of the focus has been on boys. A more recent emphasis on the numbers of black girls falling into trouble in school compared with the number of white girls who face punishment has brought to light a startling statistic: Black girls are six times as likely as white girls to draw the ire of school authorities including school resource officers.[10]

Jaws (at least those outside the black community) are dropping over the conclusions reached by recent studies on how black children are viewed. Just this summer, Georgetown University's Law Center on Poverty and Inequality published a report revealing that adults perceive black girls to be less innocent than white girls.[11] What's more, black girls are viewed through a lens that sexualizes them, portrays them as overly aggressive, and generally speaking, "adultifies" them in a way that makes it easy to hold them responsible for youthful indiscretions for which their white counterparts get a pass.

The researchers who produced the paper, titled "Girlhood Interrupted: The Erasure of Black Girls' Childhood," acknowledge that their work builds on studies showing similar adult perceptions of black boys. They note that, "In 2014, for example, research by Professor Phillip Goff and colleagues revealed that beginning at the age of 10, Black boys are more likely than their white peers to be misperceived as older, viewed as guilty of suspected crimes, and face police violence if accused of a crime."[12]

This explains why black children are so much more likely than their white peers to face punishment stemming from school-based incidents. Irrational fears and implicit bias consistently trigger selective enforcement of the rules. In the case of our protagonist, Marcus, notice that the teacher, Miss Orenstein, didn't have to directly address the widely-held fear of and disdain for black masculinity. The idea that Marcus would verbally contradict her and then pull away when she moved to physically direct him did not sit well with her. In her mind—which had been conditioned to see "Jim Crow etiquette" as the unspoken ground rules— these things added up to assault. Her subsequent performance—the outrage, the tears, and the body language of victimhood—drew upon long-existing and well-understood white damsel–big black brute trope that, in decades past, would have led to Marcus being lynched.[13]

With absolutely zero evidence, the dean immediately accepted her version of events, and used threats and intimidation to cow the boy into going to the main office. The dean followed that up by telling Marcus and Cedric that they should be prepared to empty the boy's locker under the presumption that Marcus's dismissal from school was a foregone conclusion. The dean wasn't alone in making a such a snap judgment. Even after looking at Marcus's permanent school records and seeing that he didn't have any history of discipline problems, the principal wasn't dissuaded from her initial presumption that he had assaulted his teacher.

This built-in presumption of guilt makes black children ready feedstock for the school-to-prison pipeline.[14] Worse, it fuels legal efforts to make punishments ever harsher—despite the fact that criminalizing youthful offenses such as fighting in school is not a deterrent, and typically yields discriminatory outcomes. A spot-on example of this is a Missouri law that took effect on January 1, 2017; it makes fighting on school premises a Class E felony.[15] Think about what that means. A spat between second-graders over a glue stick or colored pencils must be reported to the police. The kids involved in the fight are automatically sent to a juvenile detention center, and could face a maximum of 4 years in jail.

Before that law hit the books, a child who failed to heed the teacher's admonition to "use your words" could be charged with a misdemeanor and released into the custody of a parent. Now, it will be left to police, prosecutors, and judges to decide whether to move forward with cases that could turn seven-year-olds into convicted felons. This new level of legal jeopardy for juveniles is being applied at the whim of adults who spend their entire careers dealing with lawbreakers, and are likely to be infected with the same diseased thinking that causes society at large to view black children as older, guiltier, and more responsible for their actions than their white peers.

According to The Sentencing Project, a nonprofit advocacy group whose aim is to make the U.S. criminal justice system more just, "Like an avalanche, racial disparity grows cumulatively as people traverse the criminal justice system."[16] Police are more likely to arrest blacks than whites, given the same fact patterns. Prosecutors are more likely to charge people of color with crimes that carry stiff penalties such as mandatory minimum sentences. Judges' use of their discretion from the bench further widens the disparity. Their decisions about who is sent to jail (and for how long) versus who gets probation or judicial diversion (which lets the defendant avoid jail time and offers the added benefit of purging any record of the offense if the person stays out of trouble for a given period of time) typically fall along racial lines. A 2015 Sentencing Project report titled, "Black Lives Matter: Eliminating Racial Inequity in the Criminal Justice System," noted that even the participants in the process whose role is to actively advocate for a criminal defendant, or to present to the court a supposedly neutral recommendation about how to proceed, are biased against people of color. "A study in Washington State found that in narrative reports used for sentencing, juvenile probation officers attributed the problems of white youth to their social environments but those of black youth to their attitudes and personalities. Defense attorneys may exhibit racial bias in how they triage their heavy caseloads."[17]

Another point that shouldn't be missed is the level of representation Marcus received from the outset versus the kind afforded to most other children who find themselves accused of offenses deemed worthy of police involvement. How many parents are, like Marcus's father Cedric, skilled litigators accustomed to demanding answers? How many would have had the presence of mind to insist on actual evidence rather than acquiesce to the narrative offered early in the story by the school secretary and the dean? How many parents or guardians—many having experienced the law only as a tool of punishment or prohibition—would have entered the school building with an awareness that school administrators are as much beholden to rules (such as due process) as the students are, and are therefore obligated to show cause for their actions? Sadly, the answer is far too few. And without pushback at the moment school authorities decide how to characterize an incident, the game is all but over. Whether the outcome is suspension, expulsion, or incarceration, rarely is the avalanche of racial disparity halted once it's set in motion.

Regardless of where you fall with regard to whether Marcus should have cut through Miss Orenstein's ill-considered comply-or-die argument, you must at least acknowledge that her false accusation could have derailed his entire life. The shame is that this type of derailment occurs thousands of times each and every school day.

Cedric notes an important bit of truth: "When you're programmed to make cans, eventually you come to see everything as can-making material." The school-to-prison pipeline is a can-making enterprise that turns children into criminals, with black bodies being the most highly prized raw material. The sad lesson: Black lives matter— except for when they are under the gaze of people who, because of their positions of legal authority, have the power to kill a person's body or their dreams.

---

[1] "Are Zero Tolerance Policies Effective in the Schools?" American Psychological Association Zero Tolerance Task Force *American Psychologist* December 2008.

[2] H.R.987 - Gun-Free Schools Act of 1993. https://www.congress.gov/bill/103rd-congress/house-bill/987/text

[3] "New York City school suspensions continue to plummet, but stark disparities persist" *Chalkbeat* October 31, 2016. http://www.chalkbeat.org/posts/ny/2016/10/31/new-york-city-school-suspensions-continue-to-plummet-but-stark-disparities-persist/

[4] Ibid.

[5] Bryan Independent School District—Police in Schools Complaint. NAACP Legal Defense Fund, February 20, 2013. http://www.naacpldf.org/case-issue/bryan-independent-school-district-police-schools-complaint

[6] Isensee, L., "Feds Investigate School District for Alleged Discrimination of Ticketing African American Students" *Houston Public Media* December 10, 2013. https://www.houstonpublicmedia.org/articles/news/2013/12/10/48131/feds-investigate-school-district-for-alleged-discrimination-of-ticketing-african-american-students/

[7] U.S. Department of Education Office for Civil Rights, Data Snapshot: School Discipline, Issue Brief No. 1 (March 2014). http://ocrdata.ed.gov/downloads/crdc-school-discipline-snapshot.pdf.

[8] Bouie, J., "Are Black Students Unruly? Or is America Just Racist?" *Daily Beast* March 21, 2014. http://www.thedailybeast.com/are-black-students-unruly-or-is-america-just-racist.

[9] Ford, J.E., "The Root of Discipline Disparities," *Educational Leadership*, November 2016 http://www.ascd.org/publications/educational-leadership/nov16/vol74/num03/The-Root-of-Discipline-Disparities.aspx.

[10] Crenshaw, K., Ocen, P., and Nanda, J., "Black Girls Matter: Pushed Out, Overpoliced and Underprotected" *African American Policy Forum & The Center for Intersectionality and Social Policy Studies*, December 30, 2014.

[11] Epstein, R., Blake, J., and González, T., "Girlhood Interrupted: The Erasure of Black Girls' Childhood" *Georgetown Law Center on Poverty and Inequality*, June 27, 2017. http://www.law.georgetown.edu/academics/centers-institutes/poverty-inequality/upload/girlhood-interrupted.pdf.

[12] Goff, P. et al., "The Essence of Innocence: Consequences of Dehumanizing Black Children," 106 *Journal of Personality & Social Psychology* 526 (2014).

[13] Wood, Forrest G., "Black Scare: The Racist Response to Emancipation & Reconstruction" University of California Press 1970.

[14] Stevenson, B., "A Presumption of Guilt," *The New York Review of Books,* July 13, 2017. http://www.nybooks.com/articles/2017/07/13/presumption-of-guilt/

[15] Einenkel, W., "Missouri has a new law that makes fights in grade school a felony with up to 4 years of prison time," *Daily Kos,* April 26, 2017. https://www.dailykos.com/stories/2017/4/26/1656572/-Missouri-has-a-new-law-that-makes-fights-in-grade-school-a-felony-with-up-to-4-years-of-prison-time?detail=facebook

[16] Ghandnoosh, N. "Black Lives Matter: Eliminating Racial Inequity in the Criminal Justice System," *The Sentencing Project*, February 3, 2015. http://www.sentencingproject.org/publications/black-lives-matter-eliminating-racial-inequity-in-the-criminal-justice-system/

[17] Ibid.

Willie D. Jones has been black for more than forty years. During that time, he has done a shockingly vast number of things while black. Among them: growing up in Brooklyn, N.Y., working as a technology writer and editor for two decades, and loving his two sons (who also happen to be black). He's currently involved in a complicated, high-stakes project: helping his boys obtain a solid basic education in an America that is turning public schools into the new recruiting ground for the prison industrial complex. Will plans to continue channeling his righteous anger over the means being used to "make America great again" into books like this one.

Made in the USA
Coppell, TX
10 June 2020